Bad mood bear

John Richardson

BARRON'S

New York

"Goodnight," said Mom.
  "Goodnight," said Dad.
    But Bear didn't go to sleep.

First he played with his soldiers, then he read his picture book, and then he tiptoed out on to the landing to listen to the noise of the television.

Soon he began to feel thirsty. He went downstairs to ask for a glass of water.

"Oh, dear," said Mom.

"You'll be tired tomorrow," warned Dad.

Grandma stopped reading. And Grandad just looked at Bear over the top of his glasses and frowned.

At breakfast next morning, Bear threw his cereal on the floor.
  "Goodness me!" said Grandma Bear.
  "Good heavens!" said Mom and Dad together.

But Bear just growled. "I'm in a bad mood," he said.

Mom gathered Bad Mood Bear up in her arms and took him out into the garden.

She put him on the swing to cheer him up, but Bear had a tantrum. He fell over backwards and bumped his head.

"Stupid swing," said Bear, bursting into tears.

"Let me rub your bump better," said Mom.
 "Leave me alone," screamed Bear.
 So, Mom did.

As soon as Mom was gone, Bear picked up a big stick and hit the swing as hard as he could.

What a bad mood bear!

Bear could see Grandma and Grandad watching from the window.

He made a face.

   "That bear needs a good talking to," said Grandad.

   Grandma agreed.

"Hello, Bear," said the pigs from next door. "This is our new friend, Goat."

"So what!" snarled Bear.

"We're going down to the river to play, are you coming?"

"No. It's no fun playing with you," replied Bear rudely.

Goat said that Bear wasn't very nice and they were better off without him.

"He's not *our* friend anymore," said Pig.

Bear walked around, kicking stones and growling. A fly buzzed around his nose.

"Buzz off!" screamed Bear, flapping his arms around angrily.

Grandad was gardening in the vegetable patch and laughed to
see Bear jumping around in such a rage.

"Bad Mood Bear, calm down and stop making such a fuss!"

Bear kept right on kicking stones. He was so angry, he
didn't watch what he was doing.

"Ouch!" shouted Grandad as he fell over.

Bad Mood Bear looked up to discover he had just kicked Grandad's leg!

Dad rushed out angrily. He grabbed Bear and took him up to his bedroom.

"We've had enough of your bad mood," he said. "Behave yourself!"

Bad Mood Bear screamed and screamed. He screamed so hard that his throat hurt and his eyes ran. Then he made a few rude faces, but it wasn't much fun when there was no one there to see them.

Later on, Mom brought Bad Mood Bear a glass of milk and a cookie. Outside, a bee was humming in a sleepy sort of way. Bad Mood Bear yawned; very soon he began to feel tired.

Mom closed the curtains. Within seconds Bad Mood Bear was asleep.

Bear slept for a long, long time. When he woke up he smiled his first smile of the day.

When Mom gave Bear his fishsticks for dinner he said, "Thank you," very politely, and ate them all up.

After he had licked the bowl clean he thought about all the naughty things he had done that morning.

"I'm sorry I was a bad mood bear," he said.

Later on Bear joined his friends at the river. "Can I play too?"
he asked.

"Only if you promise not to be in a bad mood," said Pig.

"I promise," said Bear.

And he was a good mood bear all afternoon!

First edition for the United States
published 1988 by Barron's Educational
Series, Inc.

First published 1987 by Hutchinson Children's Books,
an imprint of Century Hutchinson Ltd.
London, England

© Copyright 1987 by John Richardson

All inquiries should be addressed to:
Barron's Educational Series, Inc.
250 Wireless Boulevard
Hauppauge, NY 11788

International Standard Book No. 0-8120-5871-2

Library of Congress Cataloging-in-Publication Data
Richardson, John, 1955
Bad mood bear.
    Summary: After staying up late, a young teddy bear
wakes up in a bad mood and stays mad until he takes a
nap.
    (1. Behavior–Fiction.   2. Teddy bears–Fiction)
    1. Title
PZ7439487BAD   1987   (E)   87-12653
ISBN 0-8120-5871-2

Printed in Great Britain
789   9680   987654321